STONE ARCH BOOKS
presents

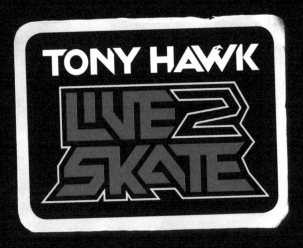

TONY HAWK
LIVE 2 SKATE

ABOVE

written by
BRANDON TERRELL

images by
FERNANDO CANO AND JOE AZPEYTIA

a
CAPSTONE
production

Published by Stone Arch Books
A Capstone Imprint
1710 Roe Crest Drive, North Mankato, Minnesota 56003
www.capstonepub.com

Copyright © 2014 by Stone Arch Books
Printed in the United States of America in Stevens Point,
Wisconsin.   032013   007227WZF13

Library of Congress Cataloging-in-Publication Data is
available on the Library of Congress website.
Hardcover: 978-1-4342-4084-2
Paperback: 978-1-4342-6186-1

Summary: When skater and filmmaker Nate Kreece loses all
his footage in a fire, he is forced to start over.

Designer: Bob Lentz
Creative Director: Heather Kindseth

Design Elements: Shutterstock.

CHAPTERS

CAMERAMAN

"Yo, man! Get your camera and let's get moving. We're late."

"Hold up, Jason. Just gimme a second to finish this."

Fifteen-year-old Nate Kreece sat hunched over the small desk in the corner of his cluttered bedroom, staring at his laptop screen. The wall behind his desk was covered in photos of pro skateboarders. Dudes like Ryan Sheckler. David Gonzalez. Even the legend himself, Tony Hawk.

He was editing a video of his friend, Zack Cross, performing a variety of skateboard tricks. On the screen now was a shot of Zack performing a switch frontside heelflip. Nate scanned through the clip and stopped it when Zack was midair, his skateboard spinning beneath his feet. He quickly dragged the clip into the editing program, saved his progress, and snapped the laptop shut.

"Is that the vid of Cross from last week?" Jason Rendell asked. He stood in the doorway of Nate's room, a battered, red deck tucked under one arm, tapping one foot impatiently.

"Yeah," Nate said. He snatched a black hoodie from a mound of clothes on his bed and slid it over his lanky frame. "Just have to add some music to it tomorrow, and it'll be done."

"Cool."

"Yeah, he has some pretty sick moves."

Nate searched his room for the gray case containing his handheld camcorder. He found it on top of a stack of *Thrasher* magazines and crammed it into his old backpack, right beside the small, red camera he usually attached to a helmet or a skateboard for first-person skate footage. Nate slung the backpack over his shoulders. Then he shoved Jason out of his room and closed the door.

The apartment Nate shared with his mom was dark and quiet. The only light came from the dining room, where

Nate had taken a break to eat a frozen pizza. Jason swiped a cookie from a jar and asked, "Your mom working late?"

"Yup," Nate answered, adding under his breath, "Again."

The two teens bounded down the apartment stairs until they reached the lobby and burst through the glass door leading outside. Without a word, they dropped their boards. They began to carve their way along the streets of downtown Chicago, weaving around walkers and cyclists. Nate flipped up his hood to protect himself from the summer wind cutting across the city from Lake Michigan.

They skated south until they reached a rundown block of wide, cement parking lots. A small group of teens, boys and girls from Nate and Jason's school, were waiting under a bridge. Some sat on their boards, while others lay on the asphalt or practiced tricks.

"What took you guys so long?" asked Zack. The tall, lanky kid wore a flannel shirt and knit wool cap. He rolled his deck back and forth under one foot.

Nate slapped him five. "Just piecing together the footage from last week," he said. "I'm trying to make you look like a halfway-decent skater."

Zack punched him lightly on the shoulder. "Ha! That should be easy, my man."

While the group warmed up by grinding rails and ollieing over cement blocks, Nate removed the gray camera case from his pack. The silver camcorder inside was his prize possession. He bought it at a pawnshop off Central Avenue using all his birthday money last year.

Nate recorded his friends for a couple of hours, getting a bunch of great footage. There was a great shot of Jason executing a nosegrind off a metal fence and a low-angle shot of Zack sailing off a cement slab, flicking his board into an epic frontside flip.

Finding adequate lighting at night was tricky, but the parking lot lights gave Nate's shots a cool, bluish hue that he really liked. At one point in the evening, some of the other crews used cans of spray paint to tag one of the bridge's colorful concrete pylons. Numerous designs and tags covered the pylon. It was a well-known spot among skaters and artists, and the city seemed okay with the vibrant designs. Nate's friends added to the artwork. They sprayed their signature logo, two skate trucks crossed in an X.

Finally, when his camera was nearly full and its battery low, Nate checked the time on his cell phone.

"Oh, man!" he said. "It's after midnight. I gotta jet."

His mom would be home from work by now, and she was totally going to freak when she found the apartment empty.

I'm gonna be grounded for at least *a month*, Nate thought.

He gathered his things and zipped up his pack. Nearby, Zack landed a 5-0 grind off a curb and shouted, "Can't wait to check out that video, Kreece!"

"I'll have it done by tomorrow," Nate said, dropping his deck to the cement and leaping on. "Swing by and I'll show it to you!" He hurriedly pushed off down the sidewalk.

Nate was two blocks from home when he heard the sirens. As he rounded the corner, he caught a strong whiff of smoke. Fire trucks and police cars were parked at the far end of the block. Their cherries lit up the night. A massive crowd of onlookers stood on the sidewalk. They watched, horrified, as firefighters battled a powerful blaze at a five-story apartment complex.

Nate nearly fell off his board.

The building engulfed in smoke and flames was his home.

Nate's first thought was: *I started the fire. I left the oven on after making my pizza. Or my computer sparked and sent a stack of stupid magazines up in flames.* Then he noticed smoke billowing from third- and fourth-floor windows. The fire had not yet reached the fifth floor, where he and his mom lived.

Mom! Sudden panic coursed through Nate's veins. He leaped off his board, kicked it up into his hands, and ran into the crowd of onlookers.

"Mom!" he called urgently. He recognized some of the tenants from his building. Mrs. Galloway in 1D. Mr. Hurley, who took out his trash twice a day. The Davis family from apartment 5C, and their cat, Fluffy.

"Mom!" Louder this time. He couldn't find her. Nate was starting to fear his mother was still —

"Nate?" Her voice came from his left. He turned and there she was, still in her work clothes. Her eyes were as wide as saucers and rimmed with tears.

When he reached her, she hugged him tightly. "Oh, thank heavens, you're safe," she said.

Nate thought the same thing. If something were to happen to his mom, he wasn't sure what he'd do.

After a long embrace, Nate's mom stepped back. She held him at arm's length. "Where were you?" she asked, sniffling.

"Out skating with Jason."

A look of disappointment flashed across her eyes, but it was quickly replaced by one of relief.

They watched for hours as firefighters worked to put out the blaze. EMTs checked on those tenants who had been inside. Meanwhile, a firefighter made sure everyone was safe and accounted for. Police officers kept everyone at a distance. Neighbors from other apartment complexes on the block offered bottles of water to the crowd. A few even took in tenants who were especially tired and upset.

Nate couldn't take his eyes off the fire. Even from his position down the street, the heat was intense. He felt numb, staring at the smoke now billowing from their windows. His whole life was disappearing right in front of him.

Finally, as the first light of morning began to creep its way across the horizon, a police officer walked over to the crowd. Behind him, the fire had been extinguished. The building was a smoking, smoldering mess.

The officer held up his hands. "If I could have everyone's attention," he said. His voice was deep and booming. "If you have somewhere to sleep and take shelter, I insist you do so now. Authorities will inform your landlord about the extent of the damage and when it's safe to return. Until then, firefighters will try to retrieve the few salvageable items from your homes."

Nate's heart dropped. *The few salvageable items?* he thought. And that was when it all hit him. He was literally left with nothing but the pack on his back. He held his skateboard close to his chest and fought hard to keep from crying.

It was a battle he quickly lost.

Later that morning, Nate sat in the backseat of his aunt
Renee's car. He listened as his mother thanked his aunt for
the umpteenth time.

"We really appreciate you and Morgan letting us stay with
you," she said.

"Of course," Aunt Renee said in a sweet, loving voice.
"We're happy to help with whatever you and Nate need."

Nate's aunt was driving them to her house in Harristown,
a city that was a half hour from Chicago. Despite the open
windows, the car smelled like smoke. It clung to Nate's
clothes and clogged his nostrils with each breath. It hadn't
even been twelve hours since they'd lost their home.

Nate's backpack sat beside him, and his skateboard lay across his lap. He spun one of the deck's dirty wheels, leaned his forehead against the cool glass of the window, and stared out at the boring 'burb.

He started listing the buildings in his head. *A strip mall. A bank. A laundromat,* he thought. *It's all so . . . flat.*

He was going to miss the towering skyscrapers, the El train, the hole-in-the-wall pizza joints. Most of all, he was going to miss his crew.

They turned into a generic housing development. *Ugh, all of the houses look the same*, Nate thought.

Finally, they stopped in front of a rusty brown, two-story home. Nate's cousin Grant was shooting hoops in the driveway. Grant was a year younger than Nate, with deep mocha skin and a solid build. The two boys didn't really hang out. They didn't seem to have much in common. Grant wiped the sweat from his forehead with one arm and waved.

Nate stepped out of the car and shrugged his pack over one shoulder. Grant stopped dribbling the ball.

"Hey, Nate," he said.

"S'up," Nate answered quietly.

"Sorry to hear what happened, dude."

Nate said nothing. He just followed his mom and aunt inside the house. They walked up wooden stairs and down a hallway. His aunt stopped at one of the bedroom doors.

"You can sleep in Katie's old room, Nate," she said, pushing open the door. "She's staying in the college dorms, so it's not a problem."

"Thanks."

"Sorry that it's a little girly," she added. She offered him a smile and squeezed his shoulder. Then she and his mother continued down the hall, and Nate entered his new room.

"A *little* girly?" he muttered to himself. It was like someone had vomited pink all over the place. The walls. The bedspread. Even the carpet. All pink. The room was still decked out as it had been when Katie lived in the house. There were photos taped to a long mirror above a white dresser. Posters of lame bands and R&B musicians covered the walls. The nightstand was even filled with bottles of fingernail polish and makeup.

Nate leaned his deck against the dresser and dropped his backpack at the foot of the bed. Then he faceplanted into the comforter. He didn't care that it was pink. He didn't care that he smelled like smoke. He hadn't slept a wink all night, and the exhaustion had finally caught up to him.

He was fast asleep in no time.

***

When Nate's eyes finally fluttered open, the pink alarm clock sitting on the nightstand read 3:35 p.m. He'd been out for five hours, give or take. His stomach rumbled; he was wicked hungry. Yet he wasn't quite ready to escape whatever safety he had in this room. He didn't want to face the world. So he sat up on the bed, stripped off his hoodie, and grabbed his backpack from the floor.

The battery for the silver camera was nearly dead, so Nate plugged the AC adapter into the wall to recharge it. Then he rummaged through his pack, lining its contents up in front of him on the comforter. The gray camcorder case. The red mini-camera. And an old, rolled-up copy of a skateboarding mag he'd forgotten was in there and some half-empty spray paint cans. That was it. That was all he owned.

Soon, there was a soft knock on the door. Nate swept the half-empty spray paint cans back into his bag. "Yeah?"

The door opened a crack, and Grant poked his head in. "You awake?"

Nate smirked. "What do you think?"

"Can I come in?"

"Your house, dude."

Grant stepped into the room and leaned against the wall. Nate could tell he was uncomfortable. Grant pointed at the silver camera still sitting on the bed. "What do you shoot?"

"Mostly skate videos of my friends."

"That's cool. You post them online at all?"

Nate shook his head. "They were all on my laptop. Back at . . . well, at what *used* to be my apartment."

There was a long, uncomfortable moment of silence. Finally, Grant broke it. "Hey, you wanna snag a bite to eat?"

Nate didn't even think about it. "That sounds awesome." He stood, stretched, and grabbed his deck.

"Bring your camera, too," Grant said. "There's someplace I want to show you."

Nate did as he was told, zipping his cameras up in his backpack. Then he followed Grant out of the vomit-pink bedroom.

Nate carved his way down the sidewalk. The familiar rattle of wheels against concrete calmed him. Up ahead, Grant rode a worn-out black BMX. He carried a super-sized cup of soda in one hand. Both boys had full stomachs. They had just finished noshing on fast-food burgers and fries.

Nate didn't have a lot to say to his cousin, but he figured small talk was a start. "So, where are we going?" he asked. It didn't really matter to him where they ended up. He was just happy to be distracted from thinking about his mess of a life.

Grant took a long pull of soda from his bent straw and said, "Infinity Skate. Harristown's one and only skatepark."

"Cool." Nate actually recognized the name. Maybe Zack had mentioned it during one of their skating sessions.

As they passed yet another strip mall – *man, this town is full of them* – Nate saw a low, white cement building. A twisted metal sculpture hung above the plain door. It showed a sideways 8, the symbol for infinity. Behind the building, an outdoor skatepark was surrounded by a black, iron fence. Nate could see a tall vert ramp as they approached.

Grant ditched his bike, and the two walked inside the cement building. Loud music bounced off the walls, which were lined with signed decks from dudes like Chris Cole and the Bones Brigade. A teenage girl with vibrant purple hair and a thick nose ring stood behind a counter.

"Day pass?" she hollered over the music.

Nate and Grant nodded. Nate dug into his pocket and withdrew a handful of crumpled bills.

"You need a deck?" the girl shouted to Grant.

"No. Just here to watch."

The girl pointed at a wall of pads and helmets and addressed Nate. "Rental gear. Helmet and pads are required." Then she vanished back into the building, swaying to the music.

Nate selected a scuffed white helmet and a set of pads.

They were still a bit damp with sweat from the last sucker who'd forgotten their gear. *Gross.*

Nate led the way into the park. It was a nice summer day, and the place was packed. Skaters took turns riding the halfpipe ramp and two clover bowls with steel coping located on the far side of the park. One of the bowls even featured a tombstone — a vertical wall on one of its curved sides.

"Dude, this place is great," Nate said as he handed Grant his backpack. "Cool if you watch my stuff?"

"Sure thing."

Grant sat on a nearby bench as Nate pulled the miniature red camera from his pack. He attached it to his rental helmet and made sure it was secure. Then he pressed the Record button and pushed off across the park.

He hit the street course first. The area was filled with rails and benches, and a few funboxes – two flat sections meeting at a raised point. Nate ollied into a 50-50 grind along one rail, a simple enough start. Both trucks locked onto the rail. The metal sung beneath his feet.

All of the pain and anger drained from him as he skated, and he was soon in the zone. He pushed off, riding up a

mini-ramp and executing a noseblunt at the coping. His front foot securely pinned the deck's nose to the ramp.

"Nice move!" shouted a teenage girl who was riding with a friend nearby. She was a bit older than Nate, with olive skin and black hair.

Instead of dropping into the bowl or fighting the crowd at the vert ramp, Nate opted to ride back to the bench where Grant was sitting. Even though it hadn't been long since they ate, Grant was munching on nachos from the concession stand.

Nate dug out his silver camera and checked the battery life. Solid green. He wasn't looking for anything specific. Still, he filmed some pretty sweet action. He found a nice angle at the vert ramp and recorded some of the skaters soaring up the transitions and performing some amazing moves. One dude nailed an invert by grabbing the coping with one hand and his board in the other. Another spun in a flawless backside 360 ollie. The skater girl who'd complimented Nate earlier rode up and did a mute grab combined with a 540, a move known as a McTwist. She was clearly one of the most talented skaters here.

Finally, as the sun lowered in the sky and the shadows in the park grew long, Nate took a few shots of the skatepark. He made sure to get a close-up of the Infinity logo out front. Then he shut down the camera and joined Grant, and the two boys rode home.

"Thanks for taking me to Infinity, man. That was just what I needed," Nate told his cousin.

It was dark outside, and they were hanging out in Grant's bedroom. Nate sat in front of Grant's laptop, uploading the footage from their adventure. Meanwhile, Grant played a football video game from a beanbag chair on the floor.

Grant jabbed at the controller, trying to complete a difficult pass. "No problem," he said, and then cursed as the opposing team's safety intercepted his pass.

Nate's footage was better than he had expected, including the first-person stuff from his helmet cam. Grant's editing software was pretty basic compared to what he was used to.

Yet Nate was still able to piece together a short, five-minute video of the park in an hour or so.

After making the final edits, he attached some music by one of his favorite indie bands to the video. Then he told Grant, "Hey, pause the game. I wanna know what you think."

Grant pressed a button on the controller, then tossed it aside and stood. Nate let him take the desk chair, opting to stand behind his cousin while the video played. It was weird, but Nate was actually pretty nervous. He cared what Grant thought of the video.

After the video was over and the screen went black, Grant let out a long, drawn-out, "Duuuude." He spun in his chair. "That was *sick*! You're, like, really good at making videos."

Nate sat on the edge of the bed. "Yeah? You think so?"

"Absolutely. And you never posted any videos of your friends online?"

Nate shook his head.

"It's totally easy. Here." He swiveled back to the laptop. Nate watched as Grant went to a popular video website for skateboarders. It was a familiar site. Nate had watched a ton of their videos for inspiration after buying his camera. Grant set up a channel under Nate's name, then selected the final clip and turned to Nate.

"Care to do the honors?" he asked with a smile.

Nate shrugged. "Sure." He leaned over the desk and navigated the laptop cursor over the site's green POST button.

With a quick click, the video was available for the world to see.

* * *

Over the next couple of days, Nate constantly refreshed the website so he could read the comments people wrote about his video. Most of them were short, like "Wicked!" or, "U rock!" or, "Insane!" Nate shot Jason and Zack a text, telling them about the website. They buzzed back saying they would check it out.

A couple of days later, while Grant was at a doctor's appointment, Nate scavenged some cash, hopped on his deck, and rode down to Infinity. This time, he brought some of Grant's old bike pads and a helmet. The same purple-haired employee worked at the counter. She barely spoke two words to Nate, just took his money and let him in.

Nate had only one camera with him this time: the red mini-cam. He attached it to his helmet, then stashed his backpack in one of the banged-up lockers lining the outside of the cement building.

There weren't as many skaters today, but Nate recognized a couple of the teens. He found some time to hit the vert ramp – spinning in an indy 360 always looked pretty killer on the helmet cam – and after, he skated in one of the clover bowls for a while.

The sun was blasting down on the concrete park, and it didn't take long for Nate to turn into a sweaty mess. He took a break, buying a bottle of water and sitting in the shade against the building. As he fiddled with the camera, a couple of teens in T-shirts and skate shorts rode up.

"Hey," one of them said, kicking his board up into his hands.

Nate looked around, then realized the kid was talking to him.

"S'up."

"You were the dude from the other day. The one filming the vert ramp. Right?"

Nate nodded. "Yeah. That's allowed, right?"

The second kid, who was taller and more muscular than his friend, shrugged. "So you posted the vid?"

Nate's heart skipped a beat. *Wait a second. These guys have seen my video?* he thought.

"Yeah."

The two teens broke out into huge smiles. "Dude, that was rad. Everybody's been talking about it."

"They have?"

"Yeah. Even Raina, the girl at the counter, has been raving about it. Her dad owns the place." *The girl at the counter? The one who barely speaks to me? Crazy.*

"So what do you charge to film somebody?" the first kid asked. "I bet a ton of amateurs looking for a sponsor would kill to have a great vid to show off their skills."

Whoa. Nate hadn't even thought of charging money for his time and talent. He shrugged. "I dunno. Guess I hadn't thought about it too much."

"Well, when you do, hit me up," the second teen said.

Then the two slapped him five and skated away across the park. Nate watched them go. His mind was reeling, and he was too amped to rest.

All he wanted to do was get back onto the course and shoot until his camera battery died.

ALL THAT'S LEFT

Nate saw his Aunt Renee's car in the driveway as he skated down the sidewalk. His mom had been borrowing the car to drive to work. She was home early today.

Excited about the events at the skatepark, Nate quickened his pace, ollied off the curb, and crossed the empty street.

He threw open the front door and rushed in. "Mom!" he shouted. He could hardly contain the excitement in his voice.

There was no answer.

"Mom!"

He heard what sounded like crying coming from the dining room. Puzzled, Nate ran through the living room and the kitchen. His mom sat in the dining room. Her elbows rested on the table, and she cupped her face in both hands. On the table in front of her was a small cardboard box. A thick, water-stained photo album sat beside it.

"Mom?"

He startled her. She used a tissue to wipe her eyes and nose, and then turned to face him. Her face was red — she'd been crying for some time.

"What's going on?" Nate asked. He walked over and sat next to her.

"I stopped and saw our landlord, Mr. Nevers, today after work," she said. Her voice was frail, brittle even. "He said the fire department had searched our apartment."

Nate looked at the box. "And this is what they found?"

She nodded and nearly broke into tears once more.

There were only a few items in the box. A couple of framed photos without the glass. A stuffed animal his mom kept on her bed, bought the day Nate was born. Nate's laptop. They were all blackened by heavy smoke damage.

"I didn't expect there to be anything left," his mother said softly. "But seeing our whole life contained in a single box somehow makes it all more difficult to . . ."

She trailed off as new tears formed in her eyes. Nate found tears were forming in his own eyes. He struggled to fight them back. He was devastated.

Finally, his mother spoke again. "We'll get through this," she told him. "We're strong, you and I."

Nate nodded. "I know."

His mom wiped a tear from his eye with her thumb.

Nate pulled the laptop from the box and carried it back to his bedroom. He didn't hold out much hope for it. So when he pressed the power button and nothing happened, he tried not to be *too* let down.

He couldn't help it, though. Anger suddenly washed over him. Nate chucked the broken laptop to the floor and quickly buried his head in one of the pillows. He cried — deep, heavy sobs that wracked his whole body. He wanted to give up, to climb on his deck and ride to the nearest pawnshop. He could sell his two cameras, get a little bit of money for them. It wouldn't be enough for his mom and him to start over, but it would help.

When he couldn't shed another tear, Nate gathered his things in his backpack. He was determined. Sure, the guys at the skatepark had said they would pay him to make a demo film. But there was no way he could make as much as he would selling the gear.

He swung open the bedroom door.

And nearly ran right into Grant.

"Whoa!" Grant stepped back.

"Sorry," Nate said. Then he noticed that Grant was carrying something. "Is that a tripod?"

Grant held it out to him. "Yeah. It was hiding out in the attic. My dad used to have a video camera, back when Katie and I were young. I thought maybe you'd want to try it out."

Nate accepted the tripod. It was heavy, with black metal legs and a flat plate at the top to screw in a camera.

And just like that, Nate's anger washed away. The thought of selling his gear was ridiculous. It was the only thing he had left. Immediately, Nate began to imagine the types of setups he could do with the tripod. It would make his framing and shots that much better.

He was going to take the teens at the park up on their offer to film them. He was going to rise like a phoenix out of the ashes of his old life and make something better for himself. Because the only thing to do after bailing off your board is to hop right back on it.

A wide smile crossed his face.

"Think you can use it?" Grant asked.

"Absolutely," said Nate. He clapped Grant on the shoulder. "Thanks, man."

IN BUSINESS

Over the next couple of weeks, Nate and Grant spent nearly every day at Infinity. The two teens who had asked him to make videos of them — Tony and Marco — made good on their promise. They paid him in cash to film them and edit together five- to ten-minute videos of the footage.

Now that he had a tripod, Nate discovered exciting new methods of filming. His pans and tilts were smooth. He would strap the tripod to his deck and roll it along the smooth cement like a camera dolly. Or he'd raise the tripod as high as it would go and shoot down from a bird's-eye view.

Grant was Nate's right-hand man. He helped during editing sessions, often finding the best take of a particular maneuver. He also designed a sweet logo of a phoenix with spread wings flying from a ball of fire. Underneath it were the words "Phoenix Videos." Nate added the logo at the end of every video, and changed the name of his webpage. At the park, Grant lugged the camera gear around and made friends with the staff and skaters. It was a sweet little operation.

One day, while Nate was setting up the tripod to get a shot of Marco doing heelflips off one of the raised platforms, he looked over and saw Grant talking to the pretty girl with sleek black hair and olive skin.

It was the girl who had complimented his skating the first day at Infinity. Nate had seen her around, but hadn't worked up the courage to ask her name yet. It seemed Grant had beaten him to it.

Nate walked over to them. "Hey, what's up?"

"Hey, Nate, this is Ione," Grant said.

"Hi," said Nate.

"Hey. I've watched your work online," Ione said. "You're pretty sick in front of *and* behind the camera."

"Thanks."

"Ione wants to shoot a video," Grant explained.

Ione added, "Yeah, I've got a couple of sponsors interested in signing me, but they want to see me in action. So I need to step up my game."

"Cool," Nate said. "What sponsors?"

Ione shrugged. "ReBoard, a recycled skateboard company from LA, and ShoveIt Shoes."

"Nice. Yeah, let's set up a time. You want to do the street course? Or the vert ramps? Or a little of both?"

"None of the above. You ever shoot anything at night?"

Nate nodded. "Yeah. It's pretty tricky, but I can make it work." He thought back to his bros in Chicago and how they would sneak out and shoot almost every night of the week. Man, that seemed like eons ago.

"Rad. I've got the perfect spot up in the city that I'd love to skate. You game?"

"Totally."

"Should we say . . . tomorrow night? I've got a car. I can pick you up here."

Nate looked at Grant, who shrugged. Nate nodded. "It's a date." He cringed. *Oh man, did I just say that?* "I mean . . . um, we'll see you tomorrow night. Cool."

Ione laughed, pushing off on her board and dropping into the nearest clover bowl.

Nate slapped himself on the forehead. "Dude. That was worse than hitting a tombstone head-on and eating concrete," he told Grant.

He watched as Ione lifted out of the pool, bending her knees and grabbing between her legs on the heelside of her board with one hand in a massive stalefish.

Things were about to get interesting.

UNDER THE EL

Nate lay on the asphalt outside of Infinity Skate and looked up at the stars. It was weird, being able to see so much of the sky. He'd grown up staring up at skyscrapers and billboards and had forgotten how overwhelming the sky could be.

From his position perched on a metal bench, Grant checked his watch. "Dude, I don't know about this. I've never gone into the city without my mom or dad."

"Relax," Nate said. "You've got a great tour guide. Besides, we'll only be gone for a couple of hours. Tops."

Nate and Grant had told their parents they were going to a late movie. But they rode to Infinity to meet Ione instead. Nate hated lying to his mom, but there was no way she'd let the two of them go into the city. And he didn't want to miss this opportunity. If things panned out for Ione, and someone important spied his video and liked it, Nate could make good money shooting for skaters all over the city.

A pair of headlights washed over them, followed by a loud, blaring horn. A rusty, blue car pulled up to the curb, and Ione leaned out of the open window. "Your chariot awaits!" she shouted.

Nate shook his head and laughed as he jumped up. Then he and Grant climbed into the car.

As they drove into Chicago, Ione plugged her MP3 player into her radio, rolled all of the windows down, and blasted punk-rock music. Nate didn't mind. He was still just amazed to be hanging out with her. In the backseat, Grant didn't seem to feel the same way. Nate caught a glimpse of his cousin in the side mirror. Grant was plugging his ears.

Finally, they reached a section of Chicago that Nate recognized. Ione drove under the El tracks and parked in a vacant lot.

An abandoned factory stood nearby. It had crumbling walls and uneven concrete, and was surrounded by a tall chain-link fence. They passed through the gate, where a sign read, "No Trespassing." As they approached the building, the El roared over their heads. The train startled Grant so much he ducked his head. Nate and Ione laughed.

While Ione warmed up, Nate filmed a couple shots of the Chicago skyline and the construction site. When the next El rattled past, he recorded that, too. These kinds of shots would give the video some context, setting the scene for Ione.

Finally, he set up the tripod, angling it to get the warehouse and the train tracks in the shot.

"See that pool of street light?" he asked.

She nodded.

"Hit your move there."

She quickly pushed off. Nate hit Record and watched as she entered the frame and rode up the side of a naturally curved cement wall. She hit a backside noseblunt by popping her deck up and stalling it at the top of the concrete.

They filmed all around the warehouse, wherever Nate could find the best lighting. Ione executed an epic noseslide by pressing the nose of her deck against a cement slab and

riding it down. Then Nate climbed a metal scaffold to record her from above. He got a sweet shot of her kickflipping into a frontside 5-0 grind on one of the scaffold's metal pipes.

As he was climbing down from the scaffold, Nate saw the blue and red lights of an approaching police car. His stomach jumped into his throat. He hurried down the scaffold as fast as he could move.

"Cop!" Grant shouted, scrambling to gather their gear.

The police cruiser stopped next to Ione's car. A tall, burly police officer stepped out, placing one hand on his hip. With the other, he shone a flashlight at the teens. Nate jumped the remaining five feet from the scaffold to the ground. The cop swung the beam of light around, shining it directly in his eyes.

"Busted," Nate muttered under his breath.

Grant's leg wouldn't stop bouncing up and down, and it was driving Nate crazy. The teens had been kept in custody at a police station on the south side of Chicago for over an hour. They were seated together on one of the uncomfortable wooden benches lining the station walls. Around them, officers bustled past or sat working at a row of desks.

Nate placed a hand on Grant's leg. "Dude. Relax." He tried to sound calm, even though his heart was struggling to hammer its way through his ribs.

"Oh, man, I'm in so much trouble," Grant whispered. He began to chew his fingernails. Ione sat passively next to him, her eyes closed, humming a tune Nate didn't recognize.

The police officer had not actually arrested them for trespassing. Instead, since it was their first offense, he'd let them off with a warning. But he had escorted them away from the factory. Then they had to ride in his cruiser back to the station to call their parents.

This was a first. In all his time skating around the city with Zack and Jason and the gang, he'd never once been busted by the cops. The other guys had — Zack alone had been fined five different times — but Nate's record was clean. Until now.

Hey, at least they didn't confiscate my camera gear, Nate thought. *Or Ione's footage.* He was thankful of that. He hugged his backpack tightly to his chest and watched the clock as the minutes ticked past.

Finally, the door to the station lobby swung open, and an officer escorted Nate's mom and his uncle Morgan back. When his mom saw him, Nate swore laser beams of rage were going to shoot out of her eyes.

"You're free to go," the officer said in a gravelly voice.

After seeing the look on his mom's face, Nate decided he was *not* relieved by that news.

The car ride home was unpleasant. Nobody spoke for the entire halfhour, which was way worse than if Nate and Grant had been yelled at by their parents. Nate could see his mom was not only angry; she was disappointed. It was the disappointment that stung. With everything they had been through recently, Nate couldn't blame her one bit.

When they got home, Nate's mom turned to the boys and said sternly, "Boys, consider yourselves grounded for one month."

"But Mom," Nate argued, "that's, like, the rest of the summer. Grant and I are making money working on videos for some of the skaters —"

"I don't care," she interrupted. "You've broken our trust. Neither of you will leave this house without myself, Morgan, or Renee knowing where you're going. And you will *not* be allowed anywhere near the skatepark. Is that understood?"

It had been a long evening, and Nate had zero fight left in him.

As one, Nate and Grant said, "Understood."

Nate quickly grew used to hanging out in the puke-pink bedroom. It wasn't *that* bad. After all, now he had plenty of time to edit Ione's footage together.

He watched a number of professional videos online, trying to determine why one was more successful than another. It was all about energy. Personality. Skill. Passion. Not only in the skater, but in the camera work, as well. You had to be unique to stand out.

Nate discovered editing was like piecing together a puzzle, finding the right moments to include in the video, and where to include them. He intercut the footage of Ione skating with shots of the skyline and the El. For some of the

sweeter moves, he changed the speed of the shot, so the board spun beneath her feet in slow motion. Editing was a challenge, but he loved every moment of it.

When Nate wasn't using the laptop to edit, Grant spent a lot of time online. He updated the videos on the Phoenix page and replied to the comments posted there.

After about a week of tinkering, Nate had a final video that he and Grant liked. But there was something missing.

He sent Ione a text: *CAN U COME OVER?*

A minute later, she responded: *B THERE IN 1 HOUR.*

By the time Ione arrived, Nate had the camera and tripod set up in the backyard. He'd placed a chair next to the brick wall of the garage.

"What's up?" Ione asked.

"I need to interview you."

"You what?"

Nate pointed at the chair. "For the video. So the sponsors can hear from you firsthand."

"I don't know . . ."

"Oh, come on. It'll be quick. Like ripping off a Band-Aid."

Ione sized him up. Then she shrugged. "Okay."

She sat down and Nate started recording. He didn't start asking questions right away, though. Ione seemed nervous, so they just talked for a while. She told him about her childhood. He told her about the fire, and about how he was shooting videos to make some money for his mom. It was nice, getting to know her like this. She was a really cool girl.

Finally, Nate asked, "So . . . why do you love skateboarding?"

Ione thought a moment. Then she said, "Why do we breathe? Eat? Sleep? Laugh? I skate because I *need to*. Because it's in my blood — it courses through my veins. Skateboarding is my passion. It's my life." She paused, then asked, "How was that?"

Nate smiled. "Perfect."

That night, Nate edited the interview footage into the rest of the video. It cut together nicely, and when Nate was finished, he thought it was the best work he'd ever done.

He burned copies of the video for Ione to send to her potential sponsors. Then, with her permission, he uploaded the video to the Phoenix webpage.

That night alone, the video had over a thousand hits.

BACK HOME

A couple of weeks before school was set to start, Nate and his mom moved out of the suburbs and back into the city. One of Nate's mom's co-workers had a fully furnished apartment she was looking to rent out. Nate's mom jumped at the opportunity. The brick, three-story apartment building was on the city's south side, not far from Nate's school.

It was weird to think, but Nate was actually bummed about leaving Harristown. The flat 'burb had changed his life. It had given him a newfound passion and purpose. He had met new friends and had grown close to Grant.

Grant and his parents rode into the city with them. In the car's trunk were a few items Nate's mom had purchased, along with some stuff his Aunt Renee was going to loan them. They spent the afternoon tidying up the place and running errands to the grocery store and hardware store for supplies.

That evening, while the adults sat talking in the living room, Nate shot Jason a text: *I'M BACK. WHERE R U GUYS?*

A minute later, his phone chirped. *THE USUAL SPOT.*

Nate snatched up his backpack and skateboard. Then he told Grant, "Come on. I want to introduce you to the crew."

They informed their parents where they were heading. "Stay out of trouble," his mom said.

Nate thought about the night he and Grant had been busted, and the look on his mom's face afterwards. "Trust me, we will," he said.

They took turns riding Nate's skateboard down the sidewalk. Grant wasn't too bad. He was wobbly and uncertain, holding his arms out at his side for balance. But he only had to bail a couple of times. Nate even taught him how to ollie.

"Look at me," Grant said. "I'm a regular Tony Hawk!"

The boys' laughter echoed through the street.

When they reached the block of parking lots, Nate saw his old crew performing tricks nearby. Zack saw him, and his face broke into a wide grin. "Well, look at who we have here!" He gave Nate a huge bear hug.

Jason approached on his deck and gave Nate a high five. "Dude, we've been following the site. Your vids are wicked good."

"Thanks," Nate said.

He introduced Grant to the gang. Then, like he hadn't skipped a beat, Nate took out his cameras. He and Grant filmed the rest of his bros. Then Grant suggested Nate jump on his deck and show off some moves. Nate handed over the camera to his cousin and joined the others.

As they were getting ready to head back home, Nate looked over at the nearest bridge pylon. There, still emblazoned on the colorfully decorated concrete, was the double truck logo they'd sprayed on it the night of the fire. Nate dug an aerosol can of red paint from Jason's stuff and walked over to the pylon.

"What are you doing?" Grant asked.

"You'll see."

Nate shook the can, and began to spray something under the truck logo. It took him a couple of minutes, and when he finished, Nate stepped back to observe his handiwork.

A bird rising up out a ball of flames.

Grant came up and stood at his side. "Nice work, Phoenix," he said.

PHOENIX RISING

Going back to Infinity Skate was like going back to Disneyworld. Ione had invited Nate to hang out, and he was pumped to see her. He hadn't spoken to her much since he'd finished the video — just a text here, a quick e-mail there.

Nate's mom drove him out to Harristown. They swung past his aunt and uncle's house to pick up Grant. Grant had with him a new set of pads, a shiny new helmet, and a mint skateboard.

"I think I'm ready to give it a shot," he said confidently.

Ione was sitting atop the metal bench outside Infinity when they got there. She ran up and gave them both big hugs. "Nice deck," she told Grant, rapping her knuckles on his helmet, which he'd already strapped onto his head.

Inside, the punk chick, Raina, was working. When she saw the trio of teens approaching, she broke into a big smile. It was the weirdest thing Nate had ever seen. "Welcome back, Phoenix!" she shouted over the blaring music.

The place was packed. It was a Saturday, and the weather was perfect. Nate attached the red mini-cam to his helmet, and then he and Ione climbed up the vert ramp. They stood on the coping beside one another. Grant stayed on the ground, opting to cheer them on while recording them with Nate's silver camcorder.

Ione turned to him. "I've got some news to share."

"What's that?"

"You're looking at the newest skater to join the ReBoard team."

Nate's jaw dropped. "No way! That's awesome!"

"Thanks. They saw the vid, and the owner called to talk to me. I'm flying out for a competition in LA over winter break."

Nate was extremely proud of his friend. She was the most passionate skater he knew, and she deserved the very best.

"Oh, there's one more thing," Ione said.

"What's that?"

A coy smile danced on her lips. "ReBoard asked me a bunch of questions about the talented dude who put together my demo reel."

Nate's heart began to race. "They . . . they did?"

"Yep. I guess they're looking for filmmakers to shoot videos of all their skaters in the Chi-Town area. The owner wanted me to give this to you."

Ione held out her hand. In it was a rectangular business card with a green recycle logo wrapped around a skateboard deck. She handed it to Nate. He was speechless.

"All right, Phoenix," Ione said, smiling. "Let's see what you've got."

She dropped off the coping and into the halfpipe. Nate turned his head to the sky and let out a loud cheer. Then he placed the business card in his pocket, hit Record on the red mini-cam, and dropped in after her.

Nate Kreece is the youngest filmmaker ReBoard employs, but you'd never know it from his footage. The only thing tighter than Nate's skating is his filmwork.

His story has inspired custom skateboard and sticker designs.

2S Above

L2S Kreece Hawk Face

L2S Phoenix

SKATE CLINIC:
OLLIE

1. Put your back foot on the tail of the skateboard and your front foot between the trucks. Bend your knees way down. The deeper you bend, the higher your ollie will be.

2. Slap the skateboard tail down with your back foot. At the same time, spring up into a jump with a quick snap.

3. As you jump, scrape your front foot up and forward along the board. This pulls the board up and guides it into position.

4. When you are high in the air, use your feet to flatten out the board under you. Level your feet on top of the board.

Bend your knees again as you head into your landing. The bent knees will absorb the impact, and the board will keep rolling forward.

SKATE CLINIC:
TERMS

5-0 grind a move where a skater pops up onto an obstacle, then grinds his or her trucks along it

50-50 grind
a move where a skater pops up onto an obstacle, then grinds his or her back truck along it and suspends the front truck above the edge

backside noseblunt
a move where a skater ollies onto an obstacle so that his or her back faces forward and grinds across it on the nose of the board

frontside flip
a move where while in the air, the skater grabs the edge of the skateboard between the trucks with the front hand. While grabbing the board, the skater then extends his or her body so the chest faces away from the board, which is pulled behind the skater. The free arm is flung out to the side.

heelflip
a move where the skater flips the board over with his or her heel

indy 360
a move where a skater places his or her back hand on the toeside of the board, while spinning 360 degrees

invert
a move where a skater grabs the board with one hand and plants the other hand on the coping of a ramp so that the rider and the board balance upside down on the lip of the ramp

mute grab
a move where a skater places his or her leading hand on the toeside of the board

nosegrind
a move where the skater grinds across the obstacle with only the front truck

ollie
a move where the rider pops the skateboard into the air with his or her feet

TONY HAWK LIVE 2 SKATE

ABOVE

By Brandon Terrell

TONY HAWK LIVE 2 SKATE

AT LARGE

By Michael A. Steele

TONY HAWK LIVE 2 SKATE

RAW

By Blake A. Hoena

TONY HAWK LIVE 2 SKATE

Strong

By Matthew K. Manning

HOW DO YOU LIVE ?

written by

BRANDON TERRELL

Brandon Terrell is the author of numerous children's books, including six volumes in the Tony Hawk's 900 Revolution series and several Sports Illustrated Kids graphic novels. When not hunched over his laptop writing, Brandon enjoys watching movies, reading, baseball, and spending time with his wife and two children.

pencils and colors by

FERNANDO CANO

Fernando Cano is an all-around artist living in Monterrey, Mexico, currently working as a concept artist for video game company CGbot. Having published with Marvel, DC, Pathfinder, and IDW, he spends his free time playing video games, singing, writing, and above all, drawing!

inks by

JOE AZPEYTIA

Joe Azpeytia currently lives in Mexico and works as a freelance graphic designer for music bands and international companies. Currently an illustration artist at The Door on the Wall studio, he enjoys playing drums, playing video games, and especially, drawing.